HI AND LOIS captures those tender, silly, helpful, ridiculous, sad, humorous, outrageous, cozy, intimate, secure, frustrating, unnerving moments experienced by many a suburban family member. The accuracy of these portrayals frequently must spark flashes of recognition among the 45 million people who read HI AND LOIS in the 800 newspapers which feature it.

The success of the strip is a tribute to its creators— Mort Walker and Dik Browne—who know whereof they write, for they are both suburbanites and fathers (Mort has seven children, Dik three).

The success of the strip may also be proof that the home is still the richest vein of human comedy and possibly the most appealing. As Mort (seven children) puts it: "My best research walks in and out of my studio all day borrowing pencils and papers!"

Hi and Lois

AMERICAN GOTHIC

BY MORT WALKER and DIK BROWNE

TEMPO BOOKS, NEW YORK

HI AND LOIS: AMERICAN GOTHIC

A Tempo Book / published by arrangement with
King Features Syndicate, Inc.

PRINTING HISTORY
Tempo original / May 1983

ISBN: 0-441-32898-9

Tempo Books are published by Charter Communications, Inc.
200 Madison Avenue, New York, New York 10016.
Tempo Books are registered in the United States Patent Office.
PRINTED IN THE UNITED STATES OF AMERICA

6-30

7-1

7-9

Hi and Lois

Mort Walker and Dik Browne

____ 17113-9	**HI & LOIS IN DARKEST SUBURBIA**	$1.25
____ 16912-6	**HI AND LOIS: BEWARE CHILDREN AT PLAY**	$1.75
____ 17008-6	**HI & LOIS: SUBURBAN COWBOYS**	$1.75
____ 16973-8	**HI AND LOIS FAMILY TIES**	$2.25
____ 16965-7	**HI AND LOIS MAMA'S HOME #6**	$1.75
____ 16986-X	**HI AND LOIS #7: FATHER FIGURE**	$1.75

Available at your local bookstore or return this form to:

 TEMPO
Book Mailing Service
P.O. Box 690, Rockville Centre, NY 11571

Please send me the titles checked above. I enclose _____
Include $1.00 for postage and handling if one book is ordered; 50¢ per book for
two or more. California, Illinois, New York and Tennessee residents please add
sales tax.

NAME _____

ADDRESS _____

CITY _____ STATE/ZIP _____

(allow six weeks for delivery)   T-9